DU

DUDLEY PUBL

D0293499

The loan of this book may be renewed if not required by other readers, by contacting the library from which it was borrowed.

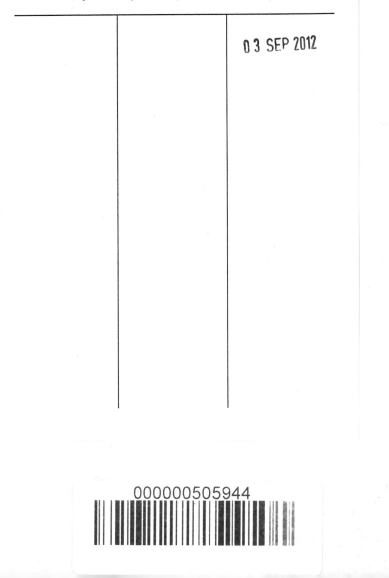

03 SEP 2012

With love to Hannah D

First published in 2011 in Great Britain by
Barrington Stoke Ltd
18 Walker Street, Edinburgh, EH3 7LP

www.barringtonstoke.co.uk

ISBN: 978-1-84299-632-4

Printed in China by Leo

Contents

Chapter 1
Island

Joe lifted his hand to shade his eyes from the sun. Down below, outside the plane window, was the bluest sea and the whitest beach he had ever seen.

The small plane circled the island as it came in to land. The holiday was the chance of a lifetime. Two weeks on a boat, sailing round the island, for a family of six. Dan and his family had asked Joe to come too. He couldn't believe his luck. He was fourteen years old

and travelling to the other side of the world –
for free.

Dan's mum, Mrs Cook to him, had won the
holiday on a TV game show. The one where
you have to guess what the dog, or the cat, or
the parrot, did next. They all watched it. Joe's
older brother gave a snort when he heard the
prize.

"You know why they've given that away,
don't you?" he'd asked. "The place is crawling
with pirates. No one wants to go there, and
who'd blame them!"

"What?" said Joe. "Like Jack Sparrow and
Long John Silver? Cool!"

Joe's brother shook his head. "This lot
carry guns, AK-47s, and Rocket Propelled
Grenades. They wear baseball caps and dirty
t-shirts. They take people hostage and kill
them if no one pays up. Nothing cool about
that."

It didn't stop Joe from going. But those words had haunted him all the way over on the plane ...

Chapter 2
Landing

"Hold tight," said the pilot as they bounced hard on the beach, rising several times into the air as the plane made a bumpy landing. Dan leant forward as if he was going to be sick.

"Use a sick bag, you muppet," said Holly, his fifteen-year-old sister. She hit him over the head, and Dan forgot his fear and sickness and slapped her back.

"Stop it, you two!" said Mr Cook. "We take you to this beautiful island and all you can do is fight. I've had enough of it!"

Joe looked the other way. These family fights made him feel really embarrassed. He wondered if they had asked him along to distract Dan from fighting with his sister. It hadn't worked. Joe didn't like Holly. She looked right through him like he didn't exist.

"One more fight and we're going to turn right around and go home," said Mrs Cook. No one really believed her.

The plane drew up by a small building at the edge of a thick line of palm trees. "Last stop, all change," shouted the pilot, like a bus driver. It was his little joke. He kept the engine running as they unloaded their bags and Mrs Cook's big straw hat blew away in the draft from the plane's propeller.

A tall, young man, with blond hair, walked slowly over to the plane. He watched Mrs

Cook's hat fly past him. Then he looked over to the plane as it sped down the hard part of the beach and into the air.

The noise of the plane faded. They could hear the lapping of waves and rustle of wind in the great green leaves of the palm trees.

"G'day," shouted the young man from half way down the beach. "Get yerselves down to the office!" he barked.

"Ooh! You're from Australia," said Mrs Cook. The young man shrugged and pointed towards the small building on the edge of the beach and began to walk over to it.

"Charming," said Mrs Cook. "Isn't he going to help us with our bags?"

They arrived, puffing and struggling with their heavy cases. As they got nearer, they could see the man was only just in his twenties.

"And who are you?" said Mr Cook, coldly.

The man took off his battered brown hat and bowed. "Nathan Driver at your service," he said with a grin. "I'm yer Captain on this little trip. Any of you got any boating experience?"

They all looked blank.

"Thought not," he said. "Never mind. Just do what yer told and watch yer hands and feet in the water. Plenty o' shark round these parts!"

They all looked shocked.

"Just kidding," he grinned. "Well, there's a few ..." He turned to Joe and Dan. "But they won't be interested in little tiddlers like you." Then he looked at Holly and winked at her. "Though you'd make a tasty morsel!"

Holly giggled and blushed a little.

"Now," Nathan said. "Let's rustle up some lunch while we wait for the boat to arrive."

He tossed a potato peeler over to Dan, who missed it and fumbled around in the sand to pick it up.

Dan looked at Joe. They were thinking the same thing. *Two weeks on a boat with this idiot. Aaagghh!*

Chapter 3
The Yacht

Nathan was a good cook, if what you liked was burgers and chips. It was lucky that they all did, apart from Dan's mum. "Got any green salad we can have with this?" said Mrs Cook.

"At once, Madame," said Nathan with a little bow. "Would you like some sushi too?"

Holly giggled.

"We don't *do* salad, Mrs Cook," he said. "It doesn't keep well out at sea."

Just as they finished their meal their yacht came sailing round into the bay. They all ran down to the edge of the beach, apart from Nathan and Holly, who were sniggering about something together.

The boat was amazing. Nearly 40 feet long, with a great tall mast. Painted white, the yacht looked sleek and slender in the gleaming blue water. It chugged towards them under the power of a small engine. The name on the back read *Angelina*.

"Ahoy there," shouted a stocky middle-aged man from the deck. "Tell Nathan to get down here, quick."

"Hi, Dad," shouted Nathan, and ran down to help tie up the boat. They all followed him, keen to get a closer look at their new home.

"I'm going at the back," said Holly.

"You're doing no such thing, young lady," said Mr Cook. "You're sharing the big cabin at the front with me and your mum. Dan and Joe are going at the back."

"Where are you sleeping?" Mrs Cook asked Nathan.

"I go in the main cabin," Nathan replied. "Close to the wheel, so I'm ready for anything."

"And what sort of anything might you have in mind?" said Mrs Cook.

"Storms, killer whales, pirates ... but normally a nice cloudless day to work on me tan!"

"Pirates?" said Joe, thinking back to his brother's warning. "Do they have pirates round here?"

"Not when I'm out sailing," said Nathan with a smile. "They wouldn't dare do anything with me in charge."

Holly looked at Nathan as if he was some kind of hero.

Joe wasn't so sure.

Chapter 4
Set Sail

When the yacht had been loaded with fresh food, oil and water, Nathan said goodbye to his dad. Joe realised then that this holiday was only run by these two men. He wondered what sort of back-up they had if anything went wrong.

Joe kept his thoughts to himself. The rest of them were so excited about the boat, even Dan and Holly had stopped fighting. Dan jumped in the warm blue water then swam round to the back of the boat. Mrs Cook was about to shout at him, then stopped. He only had shorts and a t-shirt on, after all.

Joe thought the yacht was great, but he couldn't get *that* excited about it. It was like a big caravan, and he'd been in plenty of those. The bedrooms, front and back, or *bow* and *stern* as they said at sea, were small and cosy. They had cupboards for their stuff and lockers beneath the beds.

The big cabin in the middle of the boat was all carpets and polished wood. There was a dining table, kitchen, sofas along the sides, and even a small library and music centre. Close to the main exit to the cockpit was a radio and radar.

The toilet, or 'dunny' as Nathan called it, was between the main cabin and the main bedroom. It was small but clean and smelled strongly of seawater and bleach. Directly opposite was a cramped shower room.

Holly started to rummage through the CDs propped up against the music centre. "Ozzy Osbourne? Bon Jovi? Oasis???" Her face wrinkled with distaste. "Got any grime? Any rave?"

Nathan looked puzzled. Joe gave a smirk. The Captain didn't seem quite so cool to her now.

"All hands on deck," barked Nathan once they'd settled in. They all moved out into the open cockpit behind the main cabin. Nathan was leaning on the ship's wheel.

"Now, here's the rules. I sail the ship and you enjoy yourself. Every now and then I'll ask you to help me, especially if the sea gets a little choppy. I'll ask you to wear your life jackets then, too. Got it?"

They all nodded and smiled. It seemed a good deal. Maybe Nathan wasn't so bad after all. "Oh, and I'll do the cooking," he said, "unless Mrs Cook here wants to live up to her name and do something a bit grander?"

"Can I have a go at steering?" said Dan.

"Soon as we're off the beach and out into the ocean," said Nathan.

Once the sail was lowered, Nathan pointed the bow of the *Angelina* out to the horizon. The great sail filled with air.

After half an hour, Nathan handed the wheel over to Dan. "Keep the ship due north and you can't go wrong," he said, pointing to the compass close to the wheel.

Dan handed Joe the wheel after ten minutes and he felt really excited. The wind blew warm in his face and everywhere he looked ahead was blue. Blue sky, blue sea. It was beautiful.

By the time Nathan's roast chicken dinner was cooking in the galley kitchen, the island was far away. When the meal was ready, they sat around the fold-up table in the cockpit and tucked in. It was really good. Mr Cook opened a bottle of chilled white wine and even allowed the kids to have a glass. Joe thought it tasted disgusting, but didn't say anything. He didn't want Holly to think he was still a kid.

They were all in a good mood now and even Nathan was being charming. He told them a terrible tale about some awful Americans who expected him to behave like their butler. They had even put out their shoes for him to clean during the night.

The evening sun sparkled brightly on the ocean. The sound of their voices rolled across the still water. After they'd eaten, Holly put one of Nathan's CDs on. They all banged their heads up and down and played air guitar to some heavy rock group they didn't really like.

But then Nathan stood up, looking worried, and went inside. The music stopped.

Nathan came out again with a brass telescope and a worried expression. He lifted the telescope to his eye and pointed it towards the horizon. Joe could make out a tiny speck bobbing about in the sea.

"What can you see?" said Mr Cook.

"Don't really know," replied Nathan. "But there's no other boats round here I know of."

Chapter 5

Omen

No one spoke for a few moments, then Mrs Cook suggested they turned on the radio. "BBC World Service, that's what we want," she said. "Catch up with the news."

There was a phone-in about pirates. Joe listened with a sinking feeling. "There have been several cases over the past few months where Western holiday-makers off the coast of Africa have been seized by Somali pirates," said the voice on the radio. "Large ransoms have been demanded."

"Switch it off," said Holly. "It's *bor*-ring!"

"Boring?" said Mr Cook. "It might be us!" He sounded anxious.

Nathan shook his head. "We're too far away here. They only get you if you sail too close to the African coast. Don't worry about us. No one comes this far east."

On the radio they were discussing whether the British Government should pay a ransom. A woman from Surrey came on the line. "If anyone's stupid enough to go out there, they deserve what they get," she said. "I don't want my taxes paying for their ransom. The stupid idiots."

"Switch it off," said Mrs Cook.

"Look," said Nathan. "We are hundreds of miles away from this." He sounded like he was about to lose his temper. "So stop worrying about it and have a good night's sleep."

Chapter 6
Boarded

Night fell swiftly out in the wide ocean. All around them was a darkness they had never known before. The sky was like a huge velvet blanket dotted with a trillion sparkling diamond stars. And beyond the lapping of small waves on the side of the boat, and the tinkle and rustle of the rigging, there was a great deep silence.

"Look up there," said Mr Cook to Joe and Dan as they waited, toothbrushes in hand, for

Holly to finish in the bathroom. "You can see the Milky Way." It was there, in the middle of the sky, past Gemini and Orion, and those other constellations Joe half remembered from science lessons.

The boys were lost in wonder. A huge river of stars stretching out to the rim of the galaxy. It was such an amazing sight Joe completely forgot about his fear of pirates as he fell asleep at last.

****

He woke in the night with a start. The boys had left a small port-hole window open to let in air and Joe could hear whispers, and the chink of metal outside. At first he thought it was the rigging, or Dan's mum and dad. Then he heard the squeak of a rubber boat brushing the side of the *Angelina*. Voices he did not recognise were speaking words he did not understand.

Joe leaned over to wake Dan but his friend had gone. What he did next was just instinct. Rolling off the bed, he took his sleeping bag with him and hid in the locker beneath. There were a few blankets and his backpack in there, so he wriggled to the far edge and put the sleeping bag, blankets and backpack right up against the locker door.

The bedroom door burst open. Joe heard rustling and the locker door slam open, then shut. Then there was shouting. Mr Cook saying, "What the hell's going on here?" Nathan yelling, "Calm down everyone!" Mrs Cook screaming. There was a burst of machine gun fire, then a horrible silence.

Chapter 7
Held Hostage

Joe listened intently, wondering what sort of mess he had got himself into. Who had they shot? If he came out of hiding would they shoot him? If he stayed hidden would he be able to rescue them?

Who was he kidding? What would he do against pirates with guns?

He could hear voices again. "Food!" "Water!" Urgent demands in gruff African voices.

"Here, take whatever you need," said Mrs Cook. She sounded calmer. Perhaps they hadn't shot anyone and just fired into the air?

Then he heard the men ask them all for their mobile phones. There was another scuffling of feet and younger voices too – they were talking quickly as they looked through the things they had taken.

Joe dared to open his locker door a crack and peered fearfully out into the cockpit. There were three thin figures in the moonlight. One tall man and two boys around his age. All were wearing scarves wrapped around their faces, ragged t-shirts and worn canvas trousers. They were the kind of clothes Joe's mum would have sent to a jumble sale.

The man carried a machine gun – an AK-47 by the look of it. The boys both had long knives.

Joe pulled the locker door closed again. It snapped shut with a loud click.

There was a sound of footfalls and the door was snatched open. "Don't shoot!" shouted Joe. He was terrified. "I'm coming out!"

The man reached a hand in and dragged Joe out. He flung him roughly to the deck in the cockpit and pointed his AK-47 in Joe's face.

"Don't kill me," begged Joe.

"Any trouble, we shoot you," said the man. Then he yanked off the gold chain Joe wore round his neck.

The man picked him up by the scruff of the neck. Joe could see a large black rubber boat tied to the side of the *Angelina*. Then the man hurled him into the main cabin. Joe landed with a thump, hitting his head on the side of the sofa and twisting his ankle.

The Cooks and Nathan were there. Dan and Holly were holding each other tight. Mrs Cook helped Joe to his feet and put a wet napkin against the bump that was swelling up on his forehead.

Joe was relieved to see Dan. "Where were you?" he said.

"I was in the toilet when they came aboard," said Dan. "Thought I'd hide, but they found me quick enough."

The main cabin door opened with a bang. The man said, "Who is Captain?"

Nathan spoke up. "I am. What do you want?"

"Come," said the man.

They listened to the conversation. Food … water … fuel … From what they could gather, this lot were drifting without anything to eat or drink.

"Maybe their boat's got into trouble and they just need help?" whispered Mr Cook hopefully.

Mrs Cook shook her head. "No. If they wanted help they'd have asked for it. They wouldn't need guns."

Outside, voices were rising in anger. "But that'd be murder!" they heard Nathan say.

The door opened. Nathan was thrown back inside.

"It's not looking good," he said. "They must have drifted away from the Somali coast. Maybe they ran out of fuel and got carried here by the currents."

"So what are they going to do now?" asked Mr Cook.

Another burst of machine gun fire shocked them into silence. A low hissing sound filled the air.

Nathan looked wide-eyed with fear. "He's just shot at their boat. To let the air out, so it'll sink."

"Why would they do that?" said Mr Cook.

"When we don't radio in tomorrow morning to report our position, my dad will sound the alarm. They'll send out a plane to look for us. If they see a yacht with one of those big black rubber boats tied to it, they'll know we've been boarded."

Nathan went on. "There's worse news, I'm afraid. They want to sail us back to Somalia. That could take nearly two weeks. And we've only got food and water for the next five days."

"Is that all?" said Mrs Cook.

Nathan gave a shrug. "The next island was only two days away. We had quite enough for that."

"So what are they going to do?" asked Joe.

"Throw some of us overboard," said Nathan and looked at them all in a way that suggested it wasn't going to be him.

Chapter 8
S.O.S.

"I'll talk to them," said Mr Cook. "If we can make them think we're rich, and there's a big ransom for all of us, they might change their minds."

He banged on the main cabin door. "Here, Sinbad," he shouted. "We need to talk."

The door opened and he found himself staring down the barrel of the AK-47. He reeled back as the man delivered a hefty kick to his chest.

Nathan caught him. "You need to speak to these people with a bit more respect," he hissed. "His name is Korfa. I think the boys are Nadif and Asad. Korfa speaks pretty good English. I don't know about the boys."

Korfa let Nathan finish, then pointed his gun at them. Mr Cook panicked. "Don't shoot! We're rich! We'll give you money if you don't kill us!"

A smile passed over Korfa's face. He ignored Mr Cook and stood there looking at his captives. "You." He pointed to Nathan. "Where's the lock for the door?"

Nathan went to one of the cupboards and handed him the padlock they used when they needed to lock the boat up. Korfa came in, waving his gun at them. They all backed away to the end of the main cabin. Then the two boys came in and took four large bottles of water, the remains of the roast chicken and some packets of biscuits.

The door slammed and they heard the padlock snap shut.

It was four in the morning. Nathan said, "I suppose we ought to try to sleep."

"Sleep?" said Holly. Her voice was high and thin. "How are we supposed to sleep when some of us are getting thrown overboard?"

"It might not come to that," said Mrs Cook and took her daughter in her arms.

They tried to settle down, and after half an hour a terrible tiredness swept over them. When they began to wake it was light outside and the main cabin clock showed it was half past nine.

They all listened for any sign of life in the rest of the boat. Everything was still.

"Dad should have heard from us half an hour ago," said Nathan. "So he would have called on the radio. Then he would have tried my mobile. The trouble is Korfa has got it, or one of his boys."

"I've still got my phone," whispered Joe. "I left it in the cabin here last night."

Nathan's face lit up. "Send a text to my dad," he said. "But don't make any noise. If they hear that phone bleeping you'll be in trouble."

"I left it on silent," said Joe.

There were little windows and a skylight in the cabin. "Go in the toilet," said Dan. "Where you can't be seen."

Nathan wrote down the number on a scrap of paper and told Joe what to say. Joe locked the toilet door behind him and tapped out his text:

Seized By Pirates. 150km North Grand Anse

and sent it to Nathan's dad.

Chapter 9

Ransom

The rest of the day passed in a daze. It was hot and airless in the cabin with the door locked. Nathan asked if they could open a window. But Korfa told him to shut up and said they would be beaten if they were caught talking.

So they sat and sweated and dozed and took little sips of the water they had left.

Throughout the day the pirates ran the engine and made calls on the mobile phones they had stolen. It was easy to tell when the pirates were on the phone. They would shout through the poor signal and sometimes curse wildly as each phone ran out of credit on the high charges for international calls.

Late in the afternoon they heard the lock on the door click open. Korfa put his head in, sniffed, and smiled. "Time for air," he said. "Open the skylight as well."

Fresh, salty air filled the cabin. "I have good news," he told them. "My friends come to meet us. So we have enough food and water. No one gets thrown overboard. No one walks the plank." He laughed at his own little joke.

"But I have bad news too." He paused, enjoying the fear he could see in their faces.

"When we get home, you go home too. But we want five million dollars first."

Mr Cook stood up. "But we're not rich. We can't afford five million dollars."

Korfa laughed again. "You are rich. You told me. You have this yacht! Five million, or ..." He slid a finger across his throat.

He shut the door and one of the boys slammed down the skylight.

"Now look what you've done," said Mrs Cook angrily. "I knew we should never have said anything about money!"

"No talking!" said an angry voice from outside.

Chapter 10
Plots

That evening Mrs Cook made a meal for themselves and their captors. "You eat first. We eat later," Korfa said.

"Probably thinks we're going to poison him," said Nathan, with a smirk. It was the first time he had smiled all day.

After they had all eaten, Korfa went in the stern bedroom to rest. The two boys were left to guard them. They spoke a little English and were friendlier than Korfa. They seemed afraid of him.

Nadif told them his father had been a fisherman and had to stop his work because a European ship had dumped toxic waste in the waters off the village. Asad said he wanted to be a pirate because there was no work in his village, but the pirates all lived in big houses. It was the best job in the country.

When Korfa woke up he shouted at them for talking to the hostages. He grabbed each in turn and hit them about the head.

Then he tried to use one of the two remaining phones that had credit on them.

He spoke for half an hour to someone in the pirates' village. The signal was poor and Korfa shouted for most of the time, which made it easy to hear him. Mostly he spoke in an African tongue but every now and then they could hear words they recognised, like "AK-47", "Five million dollars" and "Coast Guard".

Eventually, he used up the charge on the phone. There was one stolen phone left. Korfa powered it up, but the call charges ran out after a minute and he cursed loudly.

They heard him in angry conversation with Nadif and Asad.

"Without a phone he's going to find it difficult to arrange where to meet up with his friends," said Nathan.

"Why doesn't he use the radio?" said Joe.

"If he switches it on, the coast guard'll be able to trace the ship," said Nathan.

The door opened. Korfa had been doing some thinking. "Six of you," he said. "Five phones." He put out a hand. His meaning was clear.

They all shook their heads. No one wanted to admit they had Joe's phone hidden in the cabin. It was their contact with the outside world.

Korfa went out. Outside, they could hear the three pirates arguing. It was getting nasty.

Korfa came in again. He had given his AK-47 to one of the boys and carried a long knife. Using it to up-turn cushions and sweep the shelves of books and ornaments he turned the cabin upside down as he searched for the phone.

Then he opened the galley cupboard and pulled out the plates and pots and pans. They clattered and smashed to the floor. His prisoners shrunk back in horror, wondering what he would do next.

There was a tense silence as he looked around the room.

That was the moment Joe's phone went off. It was on silent, but its vibrations made the cupboard rattle.

Korfa dashed over and answered it. "Hi Joe," said a shrill female voice. "How are you?" It was his mum. Joe cursed himself for forgetting to turn the phone off. Korfa cut the call off without replying.

"Who is Joe?" he said in a harsh voice. "Is it you?" He held his knife to Dan's throat.

Joe stepped forward.

"It's mine," he said.

Korfa grabbed him. "Come with me."

Joe was surprised by how calm he felt. It was like some horrible glassy dream that seemed to be happening to someone else. The heat of the night hit him like a warm, damp cloth. It was no cooler outside the cabin than in.

Korfa told Asad to lock the cabin door and threw Joe down to the deck. "Kneel down," he said.

Then he grabbed his hair and pulled his head down. Joe realised that Korfa was about to cut his head off. Now everything was all too real and he felt sick with fear.

The two boys began to panic and crowded round. They argued with Korfa in a language Joe did not understand. Korfa cursed horribly then kicked Joe over. "Back inside," he said to Joe. "If I ask for anything again, you give it me, or I kill you."

Chapter 11
Bright Light

Before Korfa could open the cabin door, the boat was lit up by a fierce, bright light.

Joe was grabbed again as Korfa held him up to use his body as a shield.

"This is the Royal Navy," said a great booming voice. *"Give yourselves up."*

The boys began to panic. By their begging voices, Joe guessed they were trying to get Korfa to surrender.

"Give yourselves up or we open fire."

Korfa cursed the boys and lashed out with his free hand. Nadif and Asad made their own minds up about what to do. They both jumped overboard.

Korfa shouted out. "Don't shoot! Turn the light off or I kill the English boy!"

Joe could feel the sharp tip of Korfa's knife in the soft skin of his chin.

Korfa kneed Joe in the back. "Tell them," he hissed.

Joe shouted out. "He'll kill me! Do as he says. Please!"

The light went out.

Korfa dropped Joe to the deck and shouted, "I want five million dollars. Five million! Or I blow the boat to pieces!"

Joe thought he was making it up. So did the people on the ship.

"Surrender now or we will board you."

Korfa replied, "Switch on your light. See what I've got."

They did. To Joe's horror he could see Korfa was holding up a grenade. Korfa wrapped his fingers around the firing pin.

Two shots rang out almost at the same instant. Joe felt himself splattered with blood. Korfa's knees buckled. As he fell to the floor, Joe heard the clatter of the grenade as it fell to the wooden deck. To his horror, he could see that Korfa had pulled the pin. Without stopping to think, Joe grabbed it and threw it over the side.

The grenade exploded almost as soon as it hit the water, throwing up a huge pillar of water and pieces of wood.

"What's happening out there?" cried Mrs Cook from inside the cabin. "Joe, are you all right?"

Then he heard screaming. "*Water!*" he heard Holly shout. "It's flooding in!"

The grenade had blown a hole in the side of the *Angelina*.

"Get us out!" screamed Mrs Cook. "The water's up to our ankles!"

Joe remembered there was a tool box at the back of the boat. "Hang on, I'll try and find a crow bar," he shouted.

The Navy boat was getting closer now. "*All hands. Are you all right?*" said the voice.

"*We're sinking!*" shouted Joe.

He tugged open the tool box and searched through. There was no crowbar. Instead he grabbed a screwdriver. The *Angelina* dipped suddenly and began to tip over. Water washed into the cockpit.

"Hurry up!" cried Dan. "The water's up to our knees!"

Joe set about the lock as the sea lapped at his feet. He hacked at the lock, trying to pull it from the door. Suddenly, it gave way. The Cooks burst out, followed by Nathan.

They jumped into the water just as the *Angelina* tipped over onto her side.

Joe didn't see the big wave before it hit him, and he swallowed a great mouthful of water. But almost immediately, a Navy launch arrived to rescue them. It picked Nadif and Asad up too.

In minutes they were aboard the small navy boat HMS *Anson*, wrapped in blankets and sipping hot tea.

Holly gave Joe a great big hug. "You're a hero!" she said.

"You certainly are," said the Captain. "When this gets out, you'll be on the front page of every newspaper in Britain."

Joe didn't care about that. All he wanted to do now was ring his mum and tell her he was all right. The Captain said they could all make calls from the ship's radio room.

"I wondered why you cut me off," said Joe's mum, once she'd got over her shock at hearing such a terrible story. "Now, hang on, your brother says he has to speak to you."

Joe's brother came on the line – "Ha," he laughed. "Big brother knows best. I told you there were pirates!"

"Know all!" said Joe, and laughed along.

Joe couldn't believe he was still alive.

Barrington Stoke would like to thank all its readers for commenting on the manuscript before publication and in particular:

Ricky Black

Carly Burns

Saskia Burns

Jack Cook

Fiona Devereux

Lewis Eldridge

Tom Evans

Jose Fithill

Jake Howarth

Kieran McNamee

Andrew Muir

James Payne

Henry Pearson

Bobby Sarvagode

Mrs Bridget Smith

Nicholas Biju Thomas

Jordan Trainer

The Fall
by
Anthony McGowan

Mog might be a loser, but he's not as much of a loser as Duffy. So when Duffy tries to get in with Mog's best mate, Mog decides to take action. But when he lands Duffy in The Beck, the rancid stream behind school, Mog has no idea how far the ripples will spread...

Wolf
by
Tommy Donbavand

Adam didn't have much planned for this afternoon – head home from school, grab a snack, maybe play a video game. No way did he plan to grow some claws. Or fur. Or a tail. At this rate, Adam will be having his mum and dad for tea. And they don't seem exactly surprised...

You can order these books directly from our website at
www.barringtonstoke.co.uk

Bad Day
by
Graham Marks

Rob's going to meet Tessa.
Like, for real.
In person.
For the first time.
Then Rob starts to think
twice. And what should
have been a great day
begins to fall apart, big
style...

More fab books from Barrington Stoke

The Nightmare Card
by
Catherine Johnson

Sara wishes that she and
her best friend Mina were
more popular at school.
That's why she's come up
with a plan to tell fake
fortunes with a pack of
Tarot cards. Mina's sure
it's a bad idea. Can Mina
make Sara listen – or will
the cards take their own
revenge?

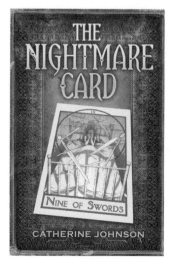

You can order these books directly from our website at
www.barringtonstoke.co.uk